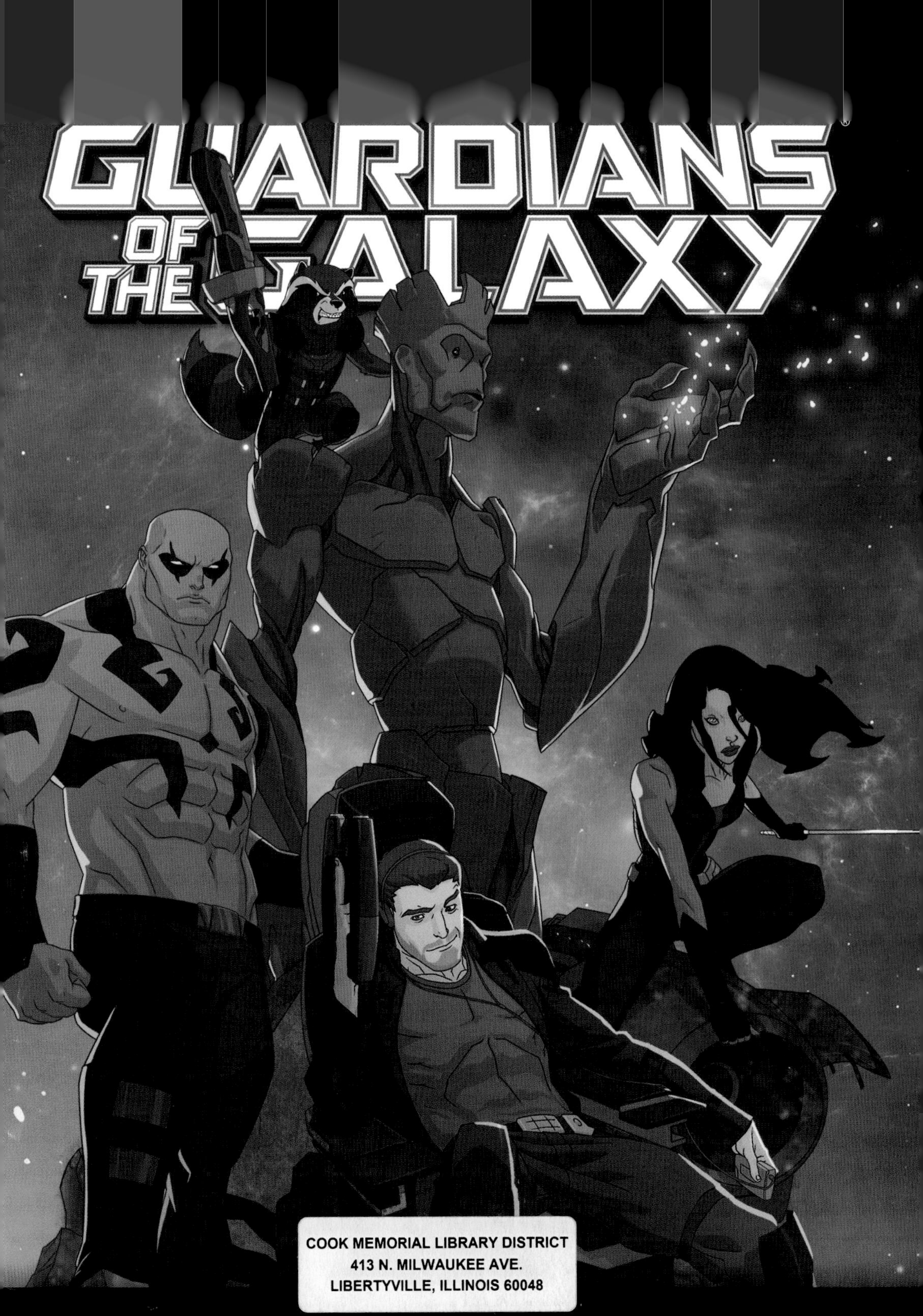
GUARDIANS OF THE GALAXY

Volume 1: Road To Knowhere

BASED ON THE DISNEY XD ANIMATED TV SERIES

Written by MARTY ISENBERG Directed by LEO RILEY
Animation Art Produced by MARVEL ANIMATION STUDIOS Adapted by JOE CARAMAGNA
Variant Cover by MICHAEL RYAN & JAVIER MENA

Special Thanks to
HANNAH MACDONALD
& PRODUCT FACTORY

MARK BASSO editor
AXEL ALONSO editor in chief
DAN BUCKLEY publisher

MARK PANICCIA senior editor
JOE QUESADA chief creative officer
ALAN FINE executive producer

ABDOPUBLISHING.COM

Reinforced library bound edition published in 2018 by Spotlight,
a division of ABDO, PO Box 398166, Minneapolis, Minnesota 55439.
Spotlight produces high-quality reinforced library bound editions for
schools and libraries. Published by agreement with Marvel Characters, Inc.

Printed in the United States of America, North Mankato, Minnesota.
042017
092017

THIS BOOK CONTAINS
RECYCLED MATERIALS

marvelkids.com
© 2017 MARVEL

PUBLISHER'S CATALOGING IN PUBLICATION DATA

Names: Isenberg, Marty ; Caramagna, Joe, authors. I Marvel Animation, illustrator.
Title: Road to Knowhere / writers: Marty Isenberg ; Joe Caramagna ; art: Marvel
   Animation.
Description: Reinforced library bound edition. I Minneapolis, Minnesota : Spotlight,
   2018. I Series: Guardians of the galaxy ; volume 1
Summary: After stealing a mysterious box from Korath, the Guardians head to
   Knowhere, but they are ambushed before they can learn more about the
   Cosmic Seed.
Identifiers: LCCN 2017931206 I ISBN 9781532140709 (lib. bdg.)
Subjects: LCSH: Superheroes--Juvenile fiction. I Adventure and adventurers--
   Juvenile fiction. I Comic books, strips, etc.--Juvenile fiction. I Graphic novels--
   Juvenile fiction.
Classification: DDC 741.5--dc23
LC record available at https://lccn.loc.gov/2017931206

Spotlight

A Division of ABDO
abdopublishing.com

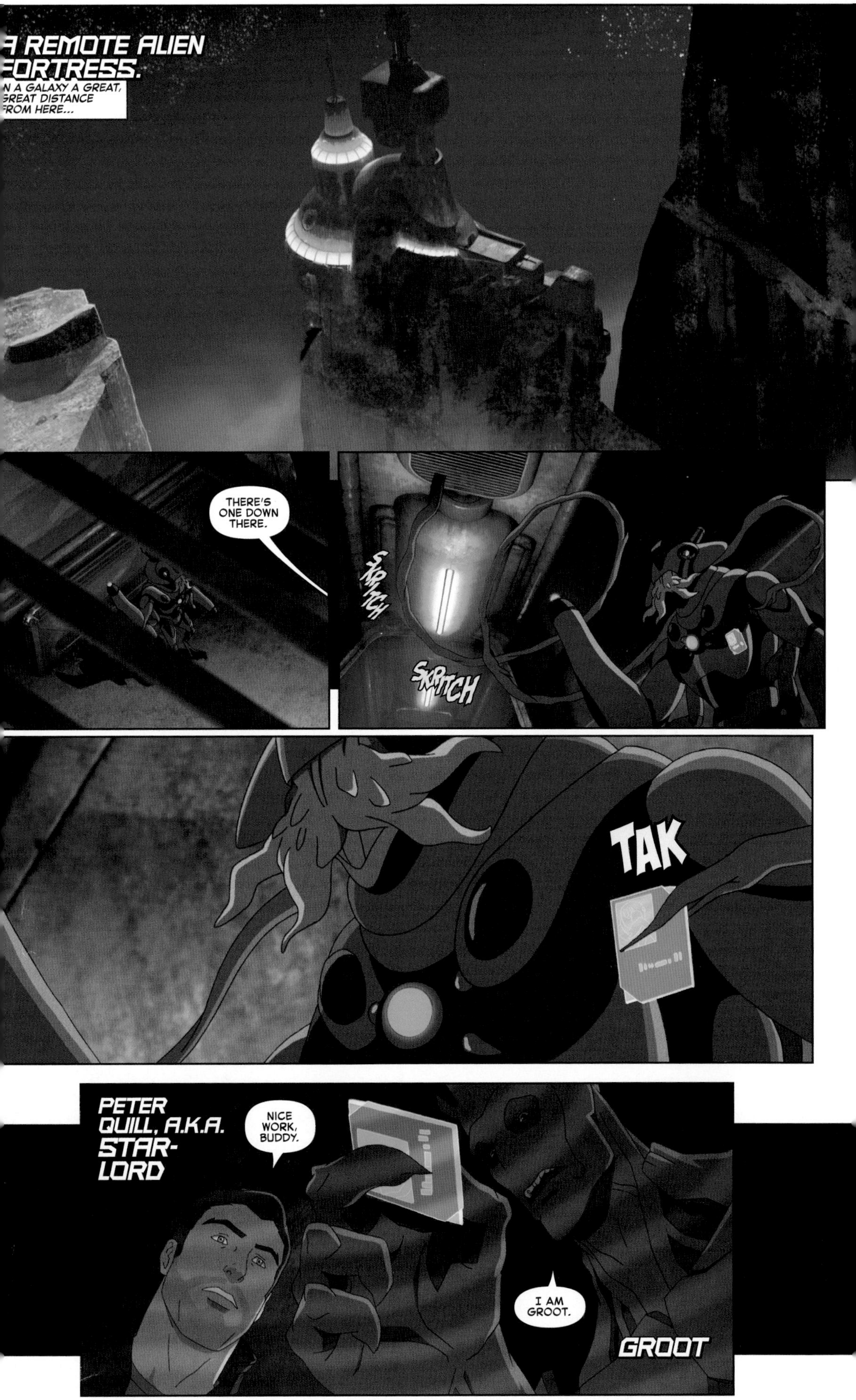
A REMOTE ALIEN FORTRESS.
IN A GALAXY A GREAT, GREAT DISTANCE FROM HERE...
THERE'S ONE DOWN THERE.
SKRITCH
SKRITCH
TAK
PETER QUILL, A.K.A. STAR-LORD
NICE WORK, BUDDY.
I AM GROOT.
GROOT

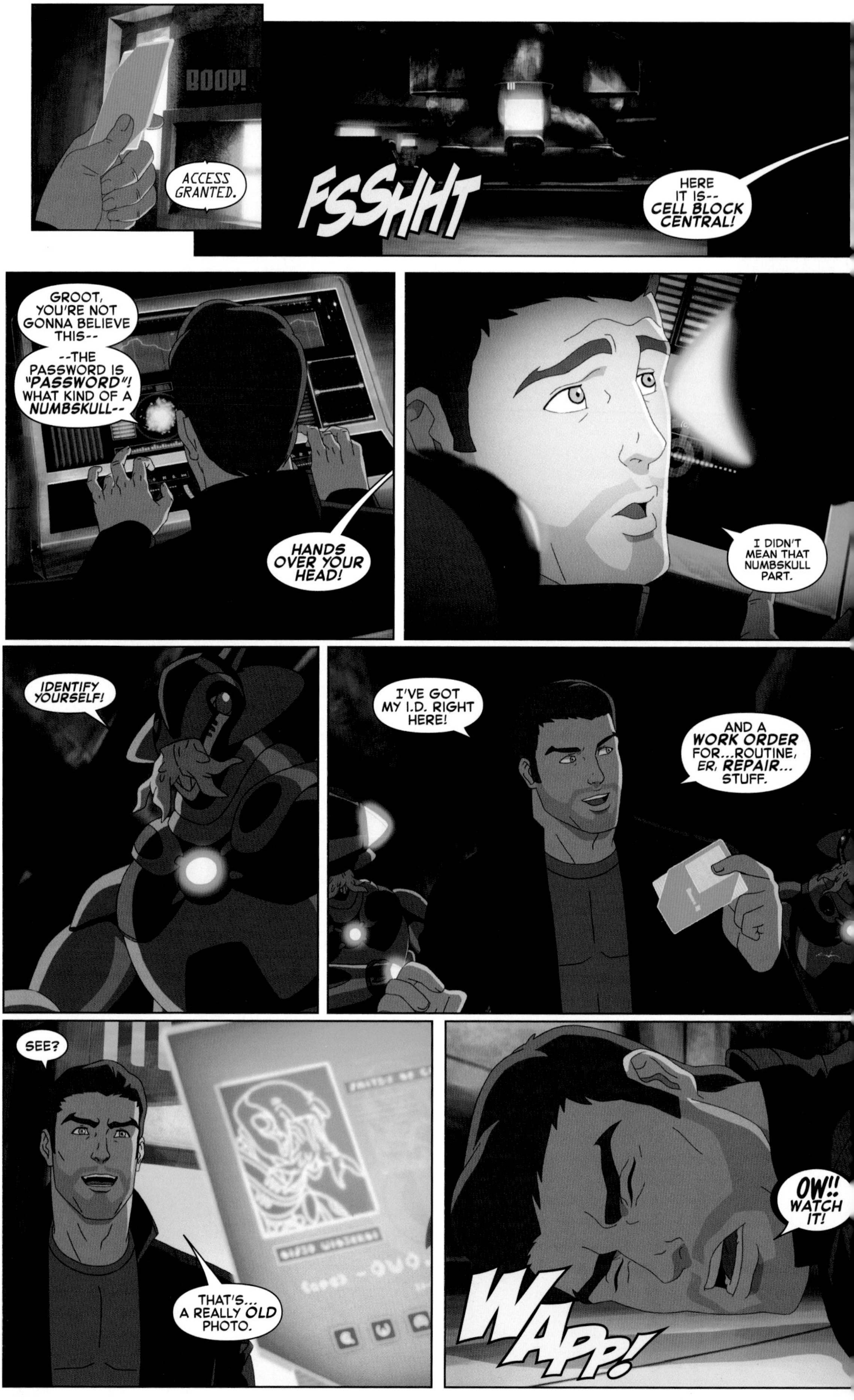
BOOP!
ACCESS GRANTED.
FSSHHT
HERE IT IS-- CELL BLOCK CENTRAL!
GROOT, YOU'RE NOT GONNA BELIEVE THIS--
--THE PASSWORD IS "PASSWORD"! WHAT KIND OF A NUMBSKULL--
HANDS OVER YOUR HEAD!
I DIDN'T MEAN THAT NUMBSKULL PART.
IDENTIFY YOURSELF!
I'VE GOT MY I.D. RIGHT HERE!
AND A WORK ORDER FOR...ROUTINE, ER, REPAIR... STUFF.
SEE?
THAT'S... A REALLY OLD PHOTO.
OW!! WATCH IT!
WAPP!

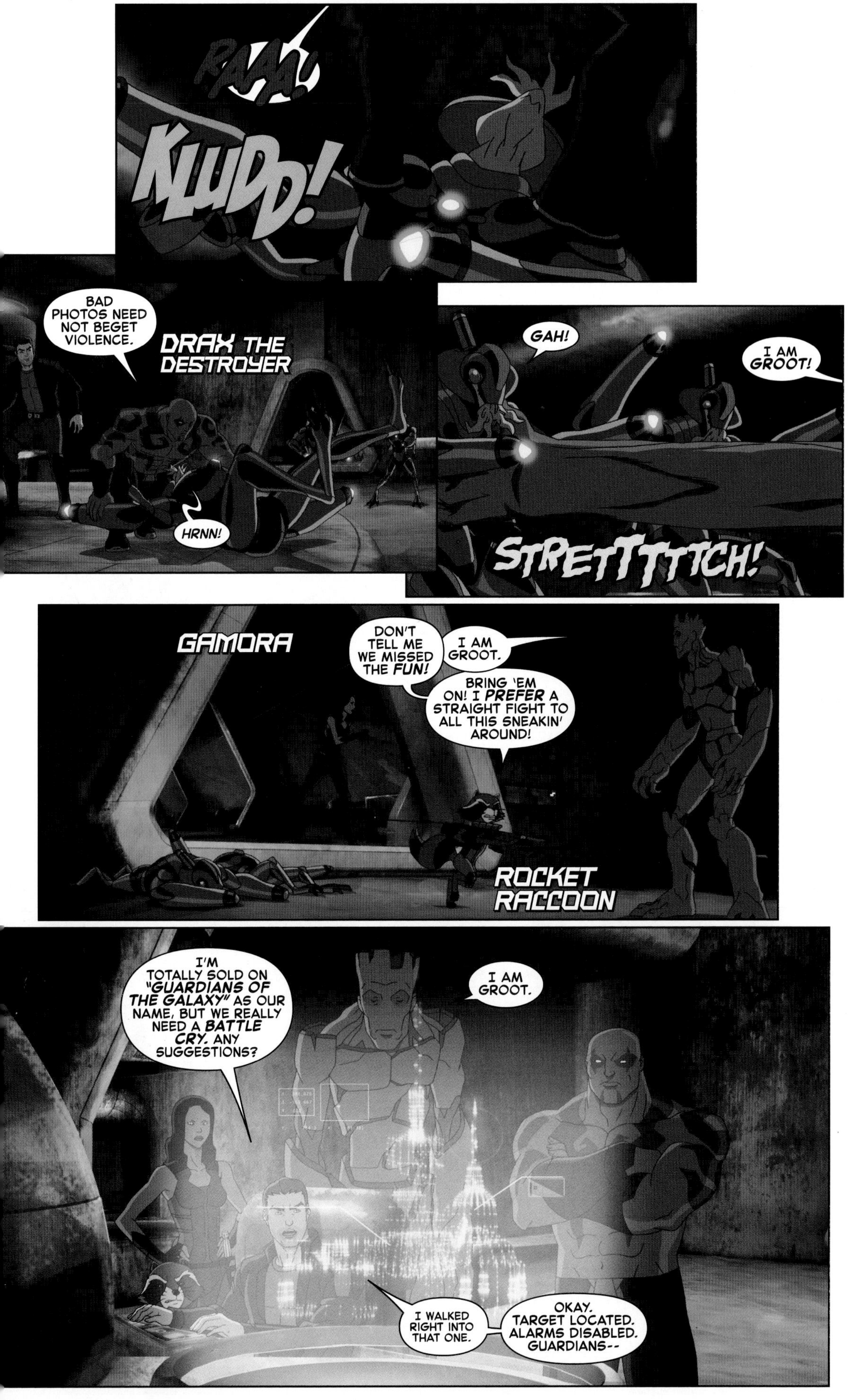
RAAA!
KLUDD!
BAD PHOTOS NEED NOT BEGET VIOLENCE.
DRAX THE DESTROYER
HRNN!
GAH!
I AM GROOT!
STRETTTTTCH!
GAMORA
DON'T TELL ME WE MISSED THE FUN!
I AM GROOT.
BRING 'EM ON! I PREFER A STRAIGHT FIGHT TO ALL THIS SNEAKIN' AROUND!
ROCKET RACCOON
I'M TOTALLY SOLD ON "GUARDIANS OF THE GALAXY" AS OUR NAME, BUT WE REALLY NEED A BATTLE CRY. ANY SUGGESTIONS?
I AM GROOT.
I WALKED RIGHT INTO THAT ONE.
OKAY. TARGET LOCATED. ALARMS DISABLED. GUARDIANS--

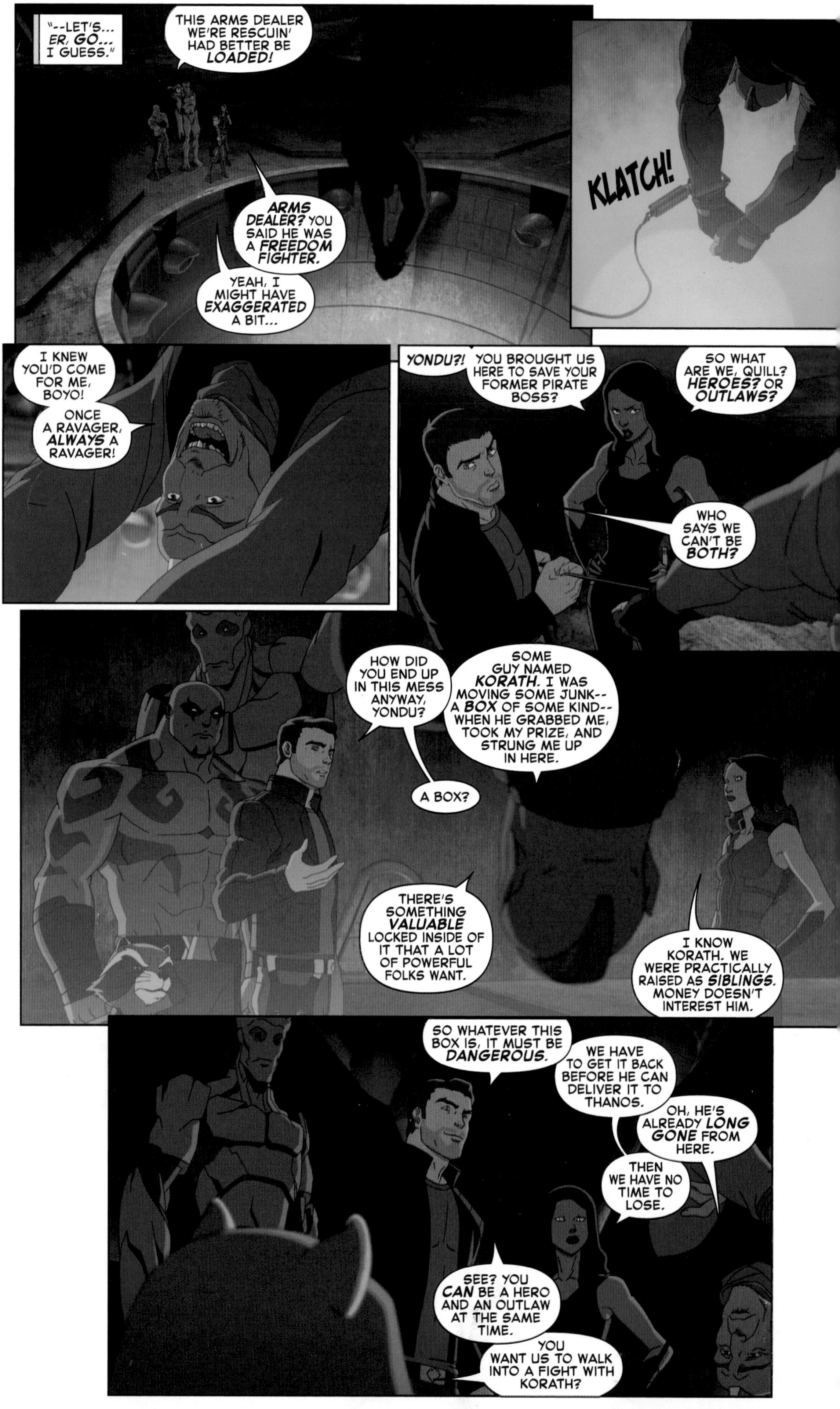
"--LET'S... ER, GO... I GUESS."
THIS ARMS DEALER WE'RE RESCUIN' HAD BETTER BE LOADED!
ARMS DEALER? YOU SAID HE WAS A FREEDOM FIGHTER.
YEAH, I MIGHT HAVE EXAGGERATED A BIT...
KLATCH!
I KNEW YOU'D COME FOR ME, BOYO!
ONCE A RAVAGER, ALWAYS A RAVAGER!
YONDU?!
YOU BROUGHT US HERE TO SAVE YOUR FORMER PIRATE BOSS?
SO WHAT ARE WE, QUILL? HEROES? OR OUTLAWS?
WHO SAYS WE CAN'T BE BOTH?
HOW DID YOU END UP IN THIS MESS ANYWAY, YONDU?
SOME GUY NAMED KORATH. I WAS MOVING SOME JUNK--A BOX OF SOME KIND--WHEN HE GRABBED ME, TOOK MY PRIZE, AND STRUNG ME UP IN HERE.
A BOX?
THERE'S SOMETHING VALUABLE LOCKED INSIDE OF IT THAT A LOT OF POWERFUL FOLKS WANT.
I KNOW KORATH. WE WERE PRACTICALLY RAISED AS SIBLINGS. MONEY DOESN'T INTEREST HIM.
SO WHATEVER THIS BOX IS, IT MUST BE DANGEROUS.
WE HAVE TO GET IT BACK BEFORE HE CAN DELIVER IT TO THANOS.
OH, HE'S ALREADY LONG GONE FROM HERE.
THEN WE HAVE NO TIME TO LOSE.
SEE? YOU CAN BE A HERO AND AN OUTLAW AT THE SAME TIME.
YOU WANT US TO WALK INTO A FIGHT WITH KORATH?

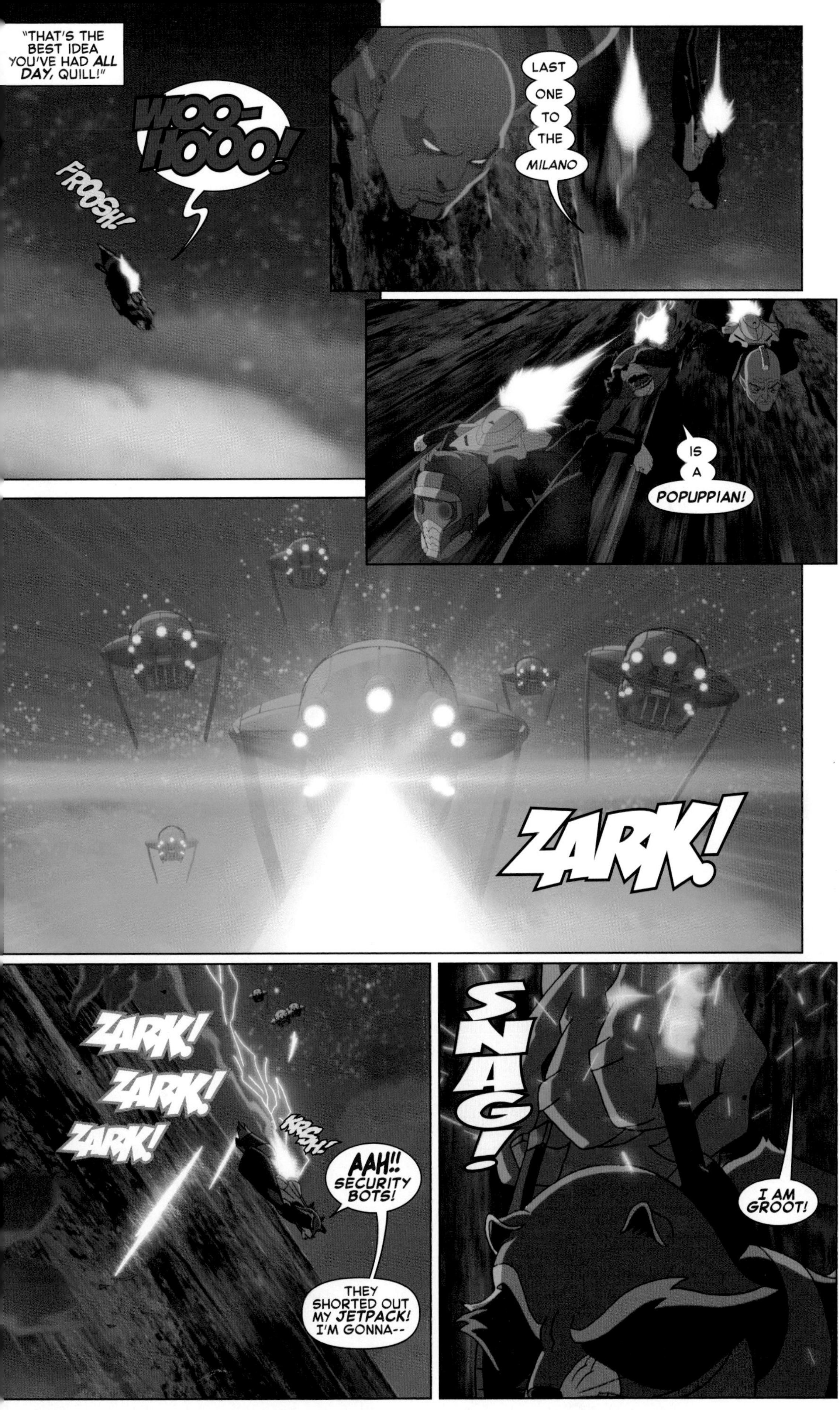
"THAT'S THE BEST IDEA YOU'VE HAD ALL DAY, QUILL!"
WOO-HOOO!
FROOSH!
LAST ONE TO THE MILANO
IS A POPUPPIAN!
ZARK!
ZARK! ZARK! ZARK!
KRSH!
AAH!! SECURITY BOTS!
THEY SHORTED OUT MY JETPACK! I'M GONNA--
SNAG!
I AM GROOT!

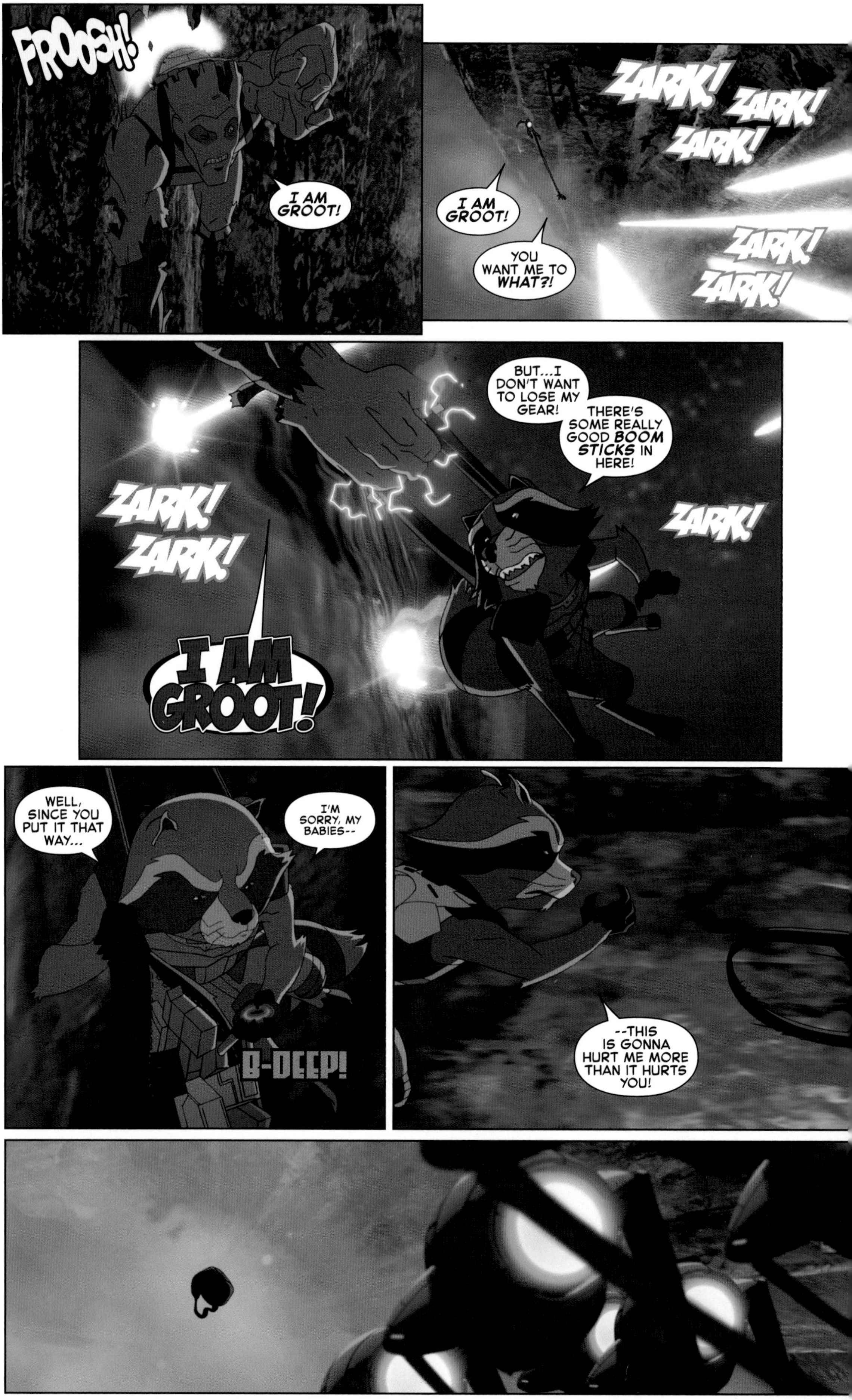
FROOSH!
I AM GROOT!
ZARK! ZARK! ZARK!
I AM GROOT!
YOU WANT ME TO WHAT?!
ZARK! ZARK!
BUT...I DON'T WANT TO LOSE MY GEAR!
THERE'S SOME REALLY GOOD BOOM STICKS IN HERE!
ZARK! ZARK!
ZARK!
I AM GROOT!
WELL, SINCE YOU PUT IT THAT WAY...
I'M SORRY, MY BABIES--
B-DEEP!
--THIS IS GONNA HURT ME MORE THAN IT HURTS YOU!

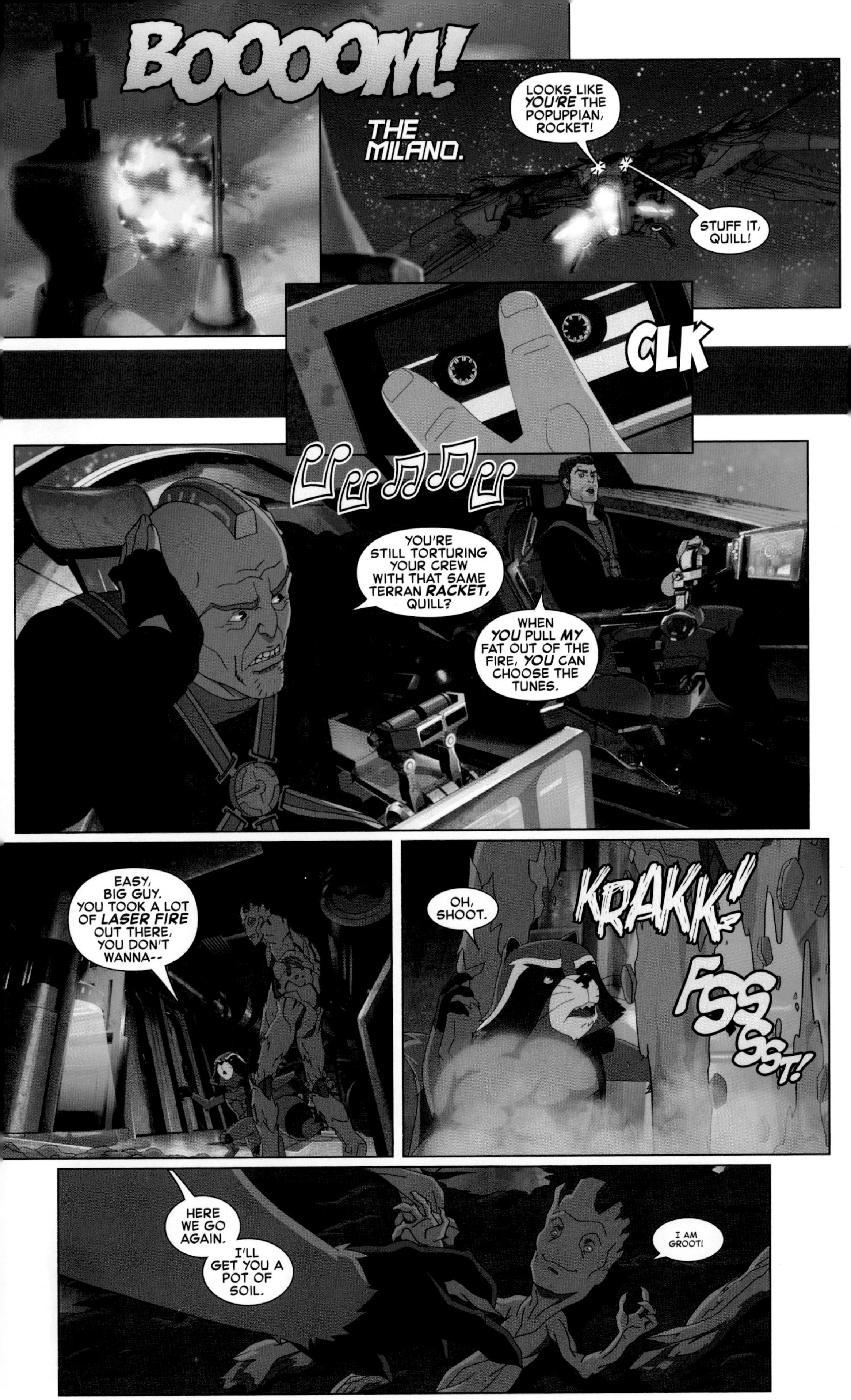
BOOOOM!
THE MILANO.
LOOKS LIKE YOU'RE THE POPUPPIAN, ROCKET!
STUFF IT, QUILL!
CLK
YOU'RE STILL TORTURING YOUR CREW WITH THAT SAME TERRAN RACKET, QUILL?
WHEN YOU PULL MY FAT OUT OF THE FIRE, YOU CAN CHOOSE THE TUNES.
EASY, BIG GUY. YOU TOOK A LOT OF LASER FIRE OUT THERE, YOU DON'T WANNA--
OH, SHOOT.
KRAKK!
FSSSST!
HERE WE GO AGAIN.
I'LL GET YOU A POT OF SOIL.
I AM GROOT!

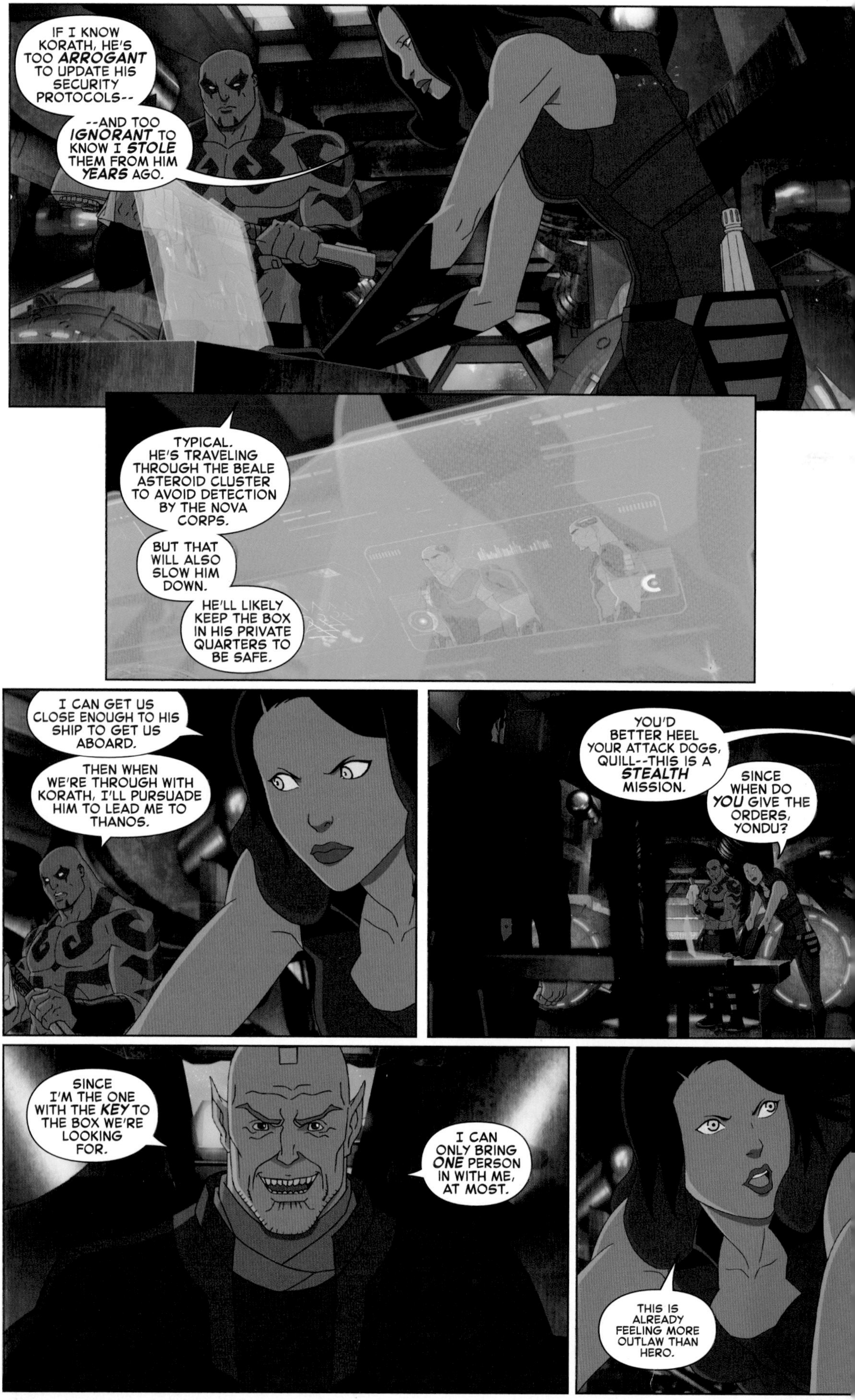

IF I KNOW KORATH, HE'S TOO ARROGANT TO UPDATE HIS SECURITY PROTOCOLS--
--AND TOO IGNORANT TO KNOW I STOLE THEM FROM HIM YEARS AGO.
TYPICAL. HE'S TRAVELING THROUGH THE BEALE ASTEROID CLUSTER TO AVOID DETECTION BY THE NOVA CORPS.
BUT THAT WILL ALSO SLOW HIM DOWN.
HE'LL LIKELY KEEP THE BOX IN HIS PRIVATE QUARTERS TO BE SAFE.
I CAN GET US CLOSE ENOUGH TO HIS SHIP TO GET US ABOARD.
THEN WHEN WE'RE THROUGH WITH KORATH, I'LL PURSUADE HIM TO LEAD ME TO THANOS.
YOU'D BETTER HEEL YOUR ATTACK DOGS, QUILL--THIS IS A STEALTH MISSION.
SINCE WHEN DO YOU GIVE THE ORDERS, YONDU?
SINCE I'M THE ONE WITH THE KEY TO THE BOX WE'RE LOOKING FOR.
I CAN ONLY BRING ONE PERSON IN WITH ME, AT MOST.
THIS IS ALREADY FEELING MORE OUTLAW THAN HERO.

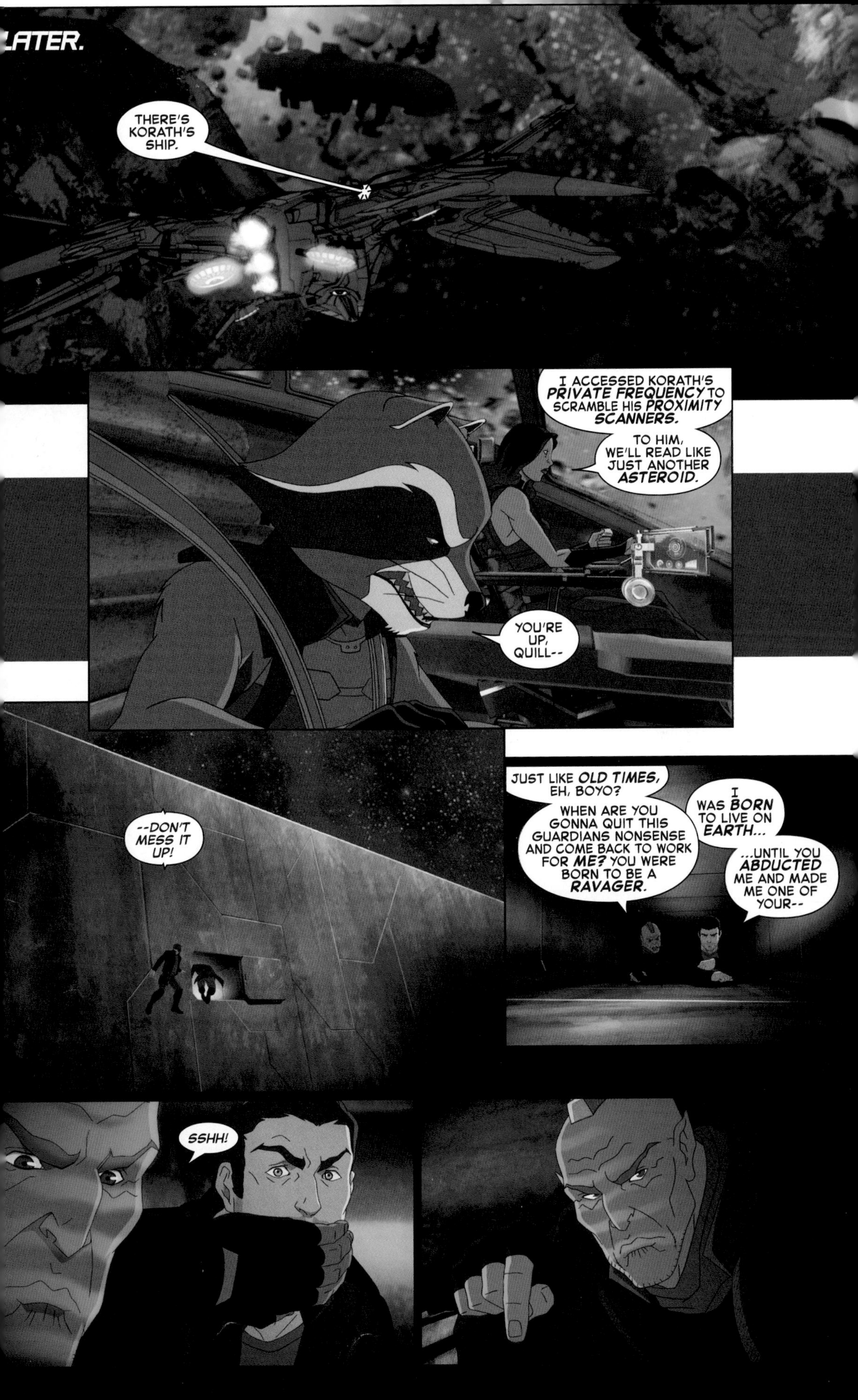
LATER.
THERE'S KORATH'S SHIP.
I ACCESSED KORATH'S PRIVATE FREQUENCY TO SCRAMBLE HIS PROXIMITY SCANNERS.
TO HIM, WE'LL READ LIKE JUST ANOTHER ASTEROID.
YOU'RE UP, QUILL--
--DON'T MESS IT UP!
JUST LIKE OLD TIMES, EH, BOYO?
WHEN ARE YOU GONNA QUIT THIS GUARDIANS NONSENSE AND COME BACK TO WORK FOR ME? YOU WERE BORN TO BE A RAVAGER.
I WAS BORN TO LIVE ON EARTH...
...UNTIL YOU ABDUCTED ME AND MADE ME ONE OF YOUR--
SSHH!

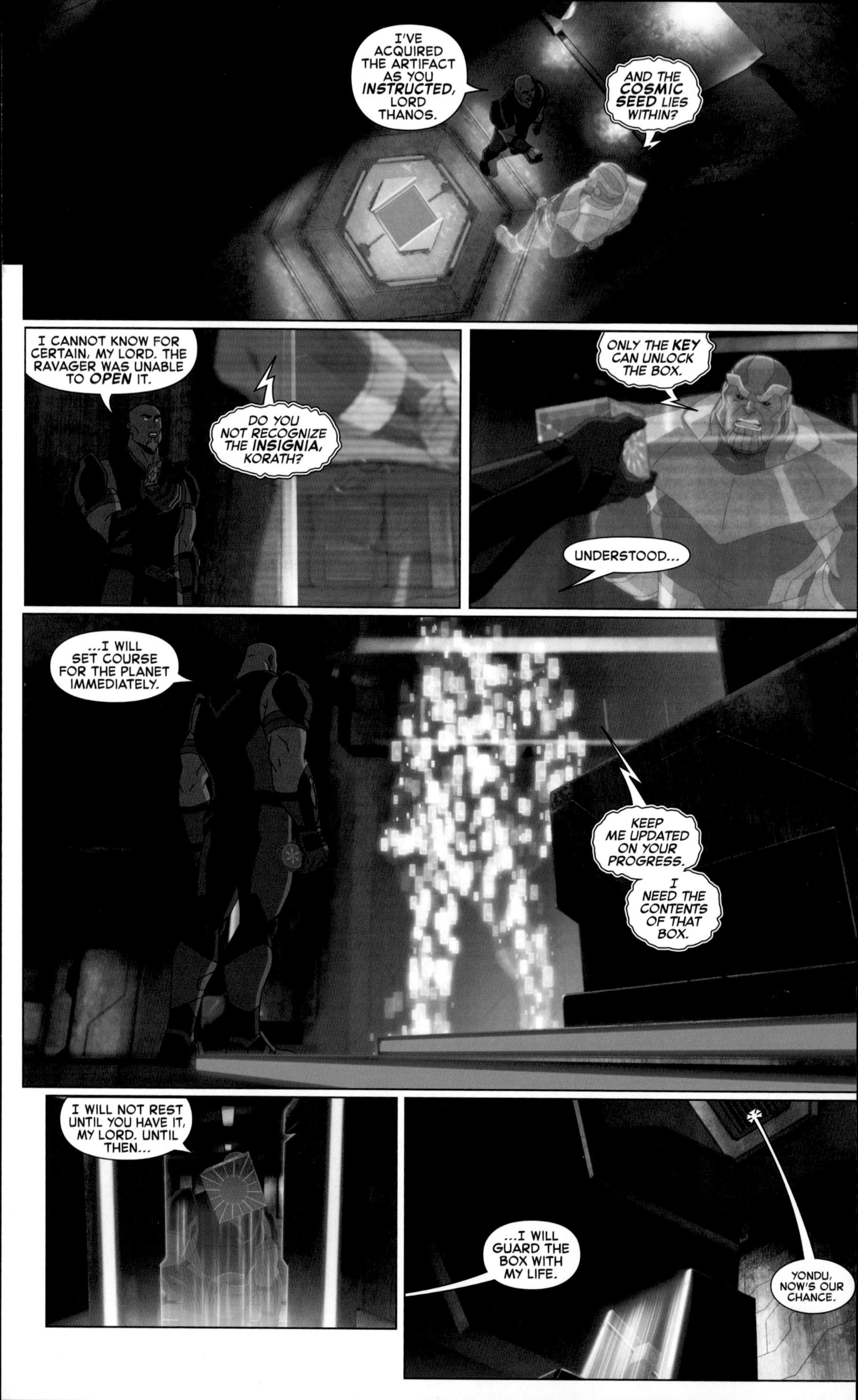
I'VE ACQUIRED THE ARTIFACT AS YOU INSTRUCTED, LORD THANOS.
AND THE COSMIC SEED LIES WITHIN?
I CANNOT KNOW FOR CERTAIN, MY LORD. THE RAVAGER WAS UNABLE TO OPEN IT.
DO YOU NOT RECOGNIZE THE INSIGNIA, KORATH?
ONLY THE KEY CAN UNLOCK THE BOX.
UNDERSTOOD...
...I WILL SET COURSE FOR THE PLANET IMMEDIATELY.
KEEP ME UPDATED ON YOUR PROGRESS.
I NEED THE CONTENTS OF THAT BOX.
I WILL NOT REST UNTIL YOU HAVE IT, MY LORD. UNTIL THEN...
...I WILL GUARD THE BOX WITH MY LIFE.
YONDU, NOW'S OUR CHANCE.

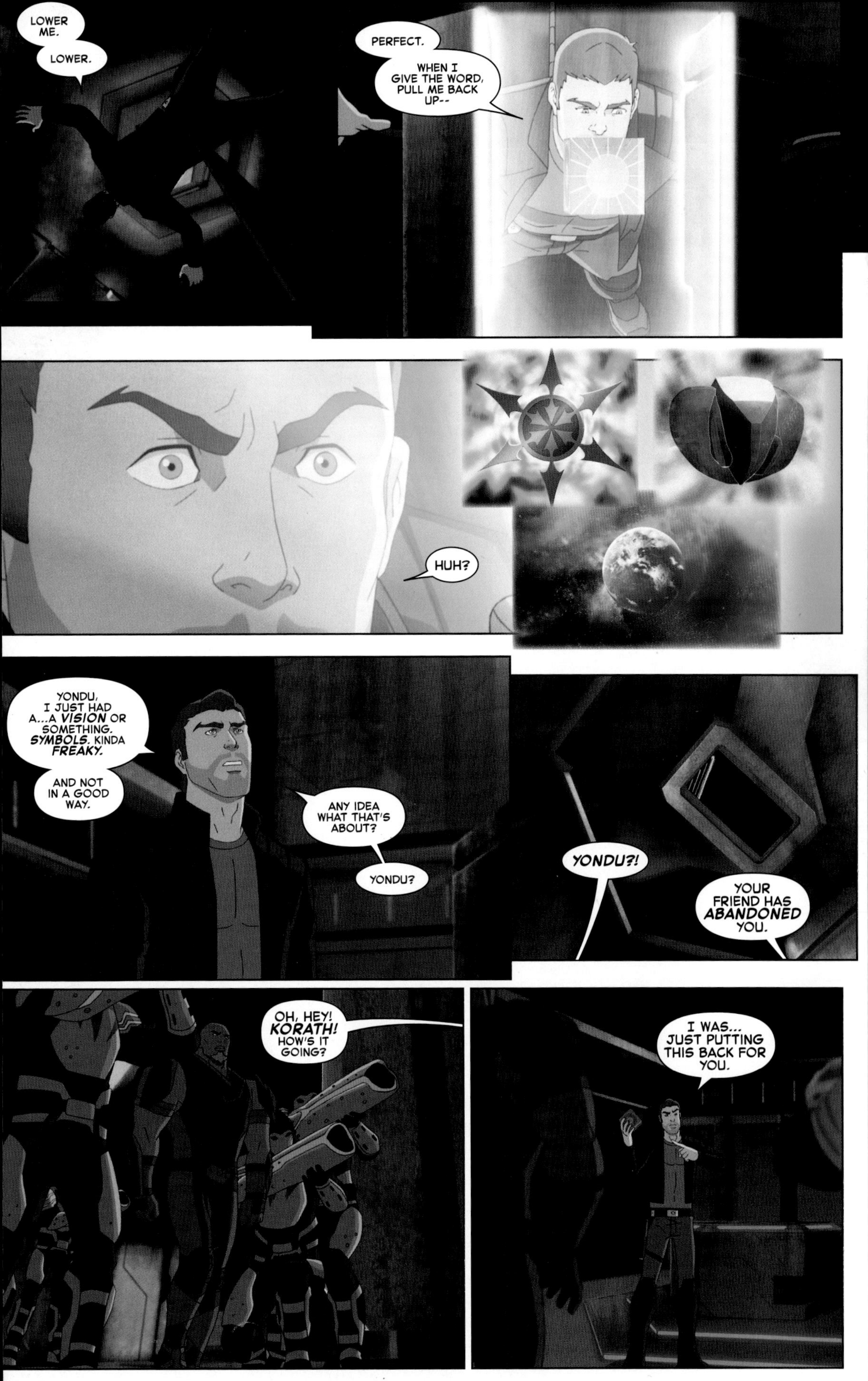

LOWER ME.
LOWER.
PERFECT.
WHEN I GIVE THE WORD, PULL ME BACK UP--
HUH?
YONDU, I JUST HAD A...A *VISION* OR SOMETHING. *SYMBOLS.* KINDA *FREAKY.*
AND NOT IN A GOOD WAY.
ANY IDEA WHAT THAT'S ABOUT?
YONDU?
YONDU?!
YOUR FRIEND HAS *ABANDONED* YOU.
OH, HEY! *KORATH!* HOW'S IT GOING?
I WAS... JUST PUTTING THIS BACK FOR YOU.

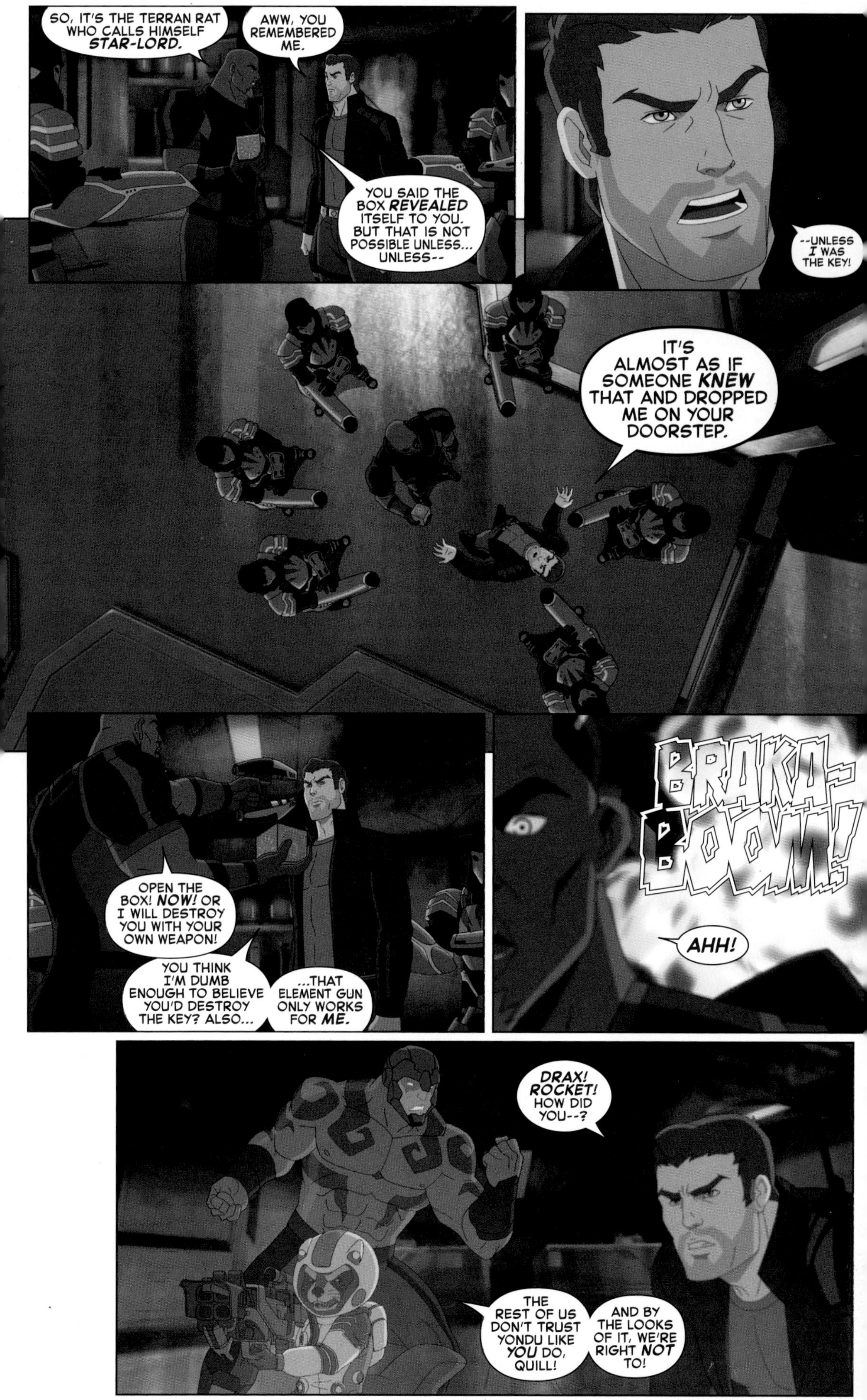

SO, IT'S THE TERRAN RAT WHO CALLS HIMSELF STAR-LORD.
AWW, YOU REMEMBERED ME.
YOU SAID THE BOX REVEALED ITSELF TO YOU. BUT THAT IS NOT POSSIBLE UNLESS... UNLESS--
--UNLESS I WAS THE KEY!
IT'S ALMOST AS IF SOMEONE KNEW THAT AND DROPPED ME ON YOUR DOORSTEP.
OPEN THE BOX! NOW! OR I WILL DESTROY YOU WITH YOUR OWN WEAPON!
YOU THINK I'M DUMB ENOUGH TO BELIEVE YOU'D DESTROY THE KEY? ALSO...
...THAT ELEMENT GUN ONLY WORKS FOR ME.
BRAKA-BOOM!
AHH!
DRAX! ROCKET! HOW DID YOU--?
THE REST OF US DON'T TRUST YONDU LIKE YOU DO, QUILL!
AND BY THE LOOKS OF IT, WE'RE RIGHT NOT TO!

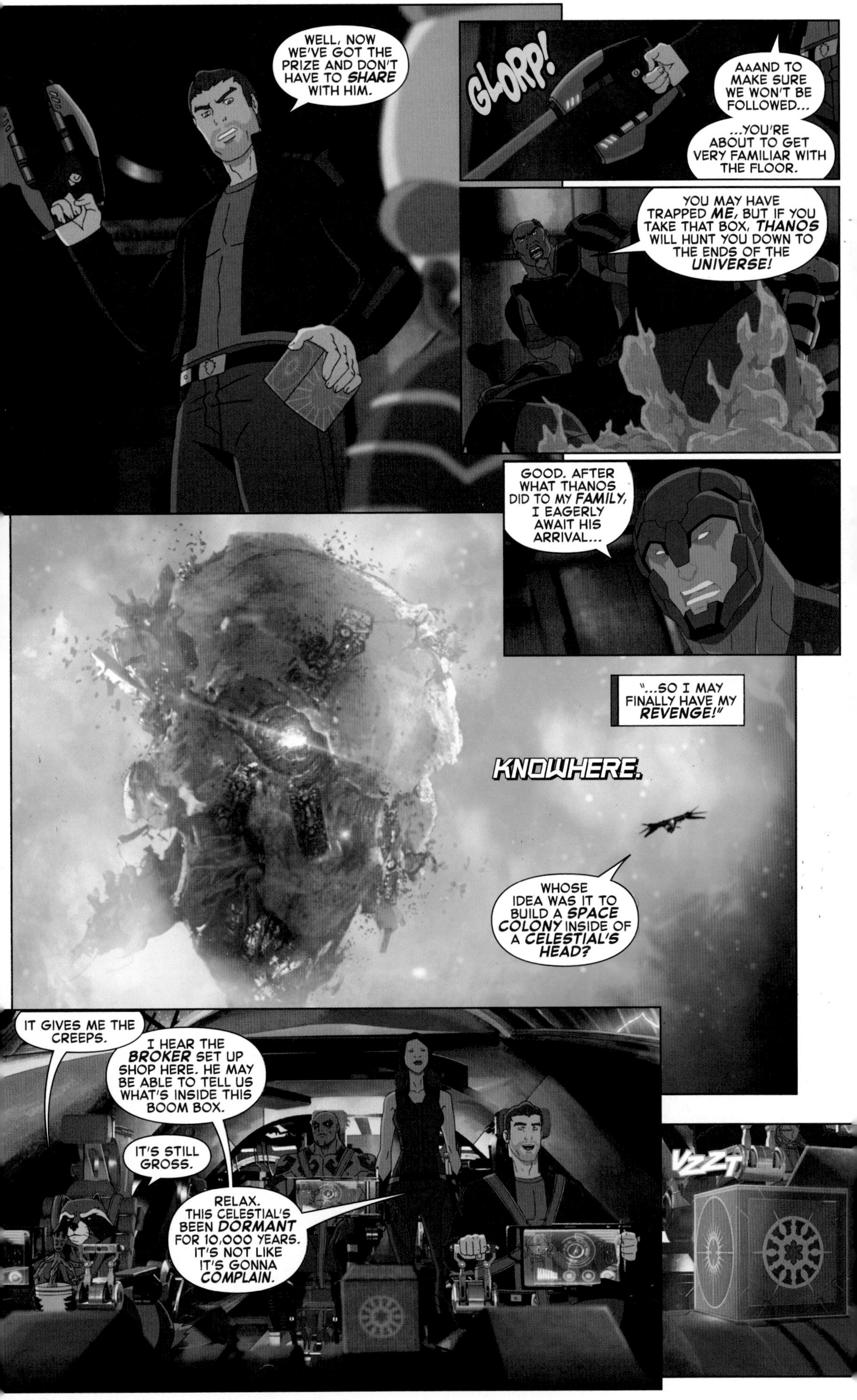
WELL, NOW WE'VE GOT THE PRIZE AND DON'T HAVE TO SHARE WITH HIM.
GLORP!
AAAND TO MAKE SURE WE WON'T BE FOLLOWED...
...YOU'RE ABOUT TO GET VERY FAMILIAR WITH THE FLOOR.
YOU MAY HAVE TRAPPED ME, BUT IF YOU TAKE THAT BOX, THANOS WILL HUNT YOU DOWN TO THE ENDS OF THE UNIVERSE!
GOOD. AFTER WHAT THANOS DID TO MY FAMILY, I EAGERLY AWAIT HIS ARRIVAL...
"...SO I MAY FINALLY HAVE MY REVENGE!"
KNOWHERE.
WHOSE IDEA WAS IT TO BUILD A SPACE COLONY INSIDE OF A CELESTIAL'S HEAD?
IT GIVES ME THE CREEPS.
I HEAR THE BROKER SET UP SHOP HERE. HE MAY BE ABLE TO TELL US WHAT'S INSIDE THIS BOOM BOX.
IT'S STILL GROSS.
RELAX. THIS CELESTIAL'S BEEN DORMANT FOR 10,000 YEARS. IT'S NOT LIKE IT'S GONNA COMPLAIN.
VZZT

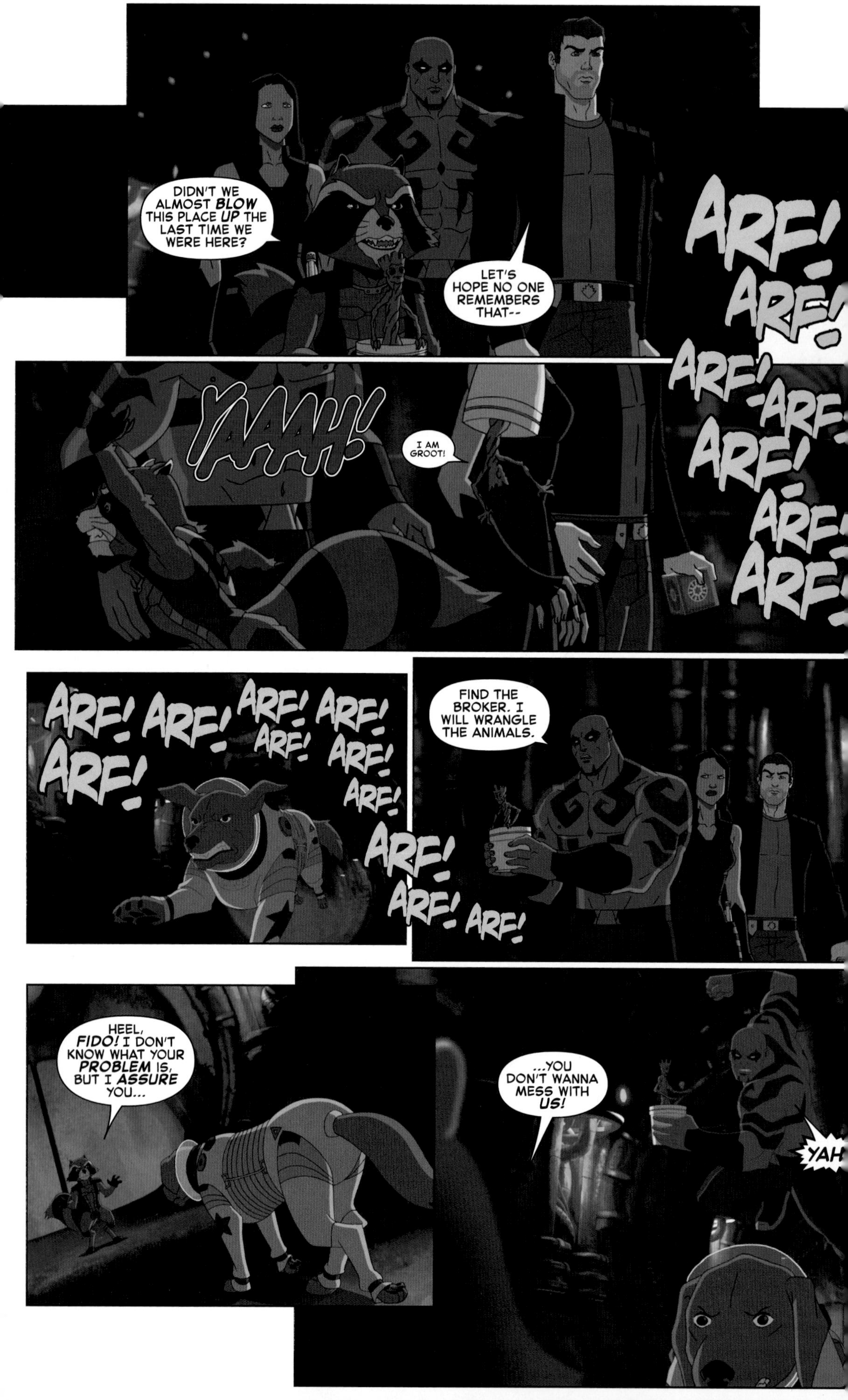
DIDN'T WE ALMOST BLOW THIS PLACE UP THE LAST TIME WE WERE HERE?
LET'S HOPE NO ONE REMEMBERS THAT--
ARF! ARF! ARF! ARF! ARF! ARF! ARF!
YAAAH!
I AM GROOT!
ARF! ARF! ARF! ARF! ARF! ARF! ARF! ARF! ARF! ARF! ARF!
FIND THE BROKER. I WILL WRANGLE THE ANIMALS.
HEEL, FIDO! I DON'T KNOW WHAT YOUR PROBLEM IS, BUT I ASSURE YOU...
...YOU DON'T WANNA MESS WITH US!
YAH

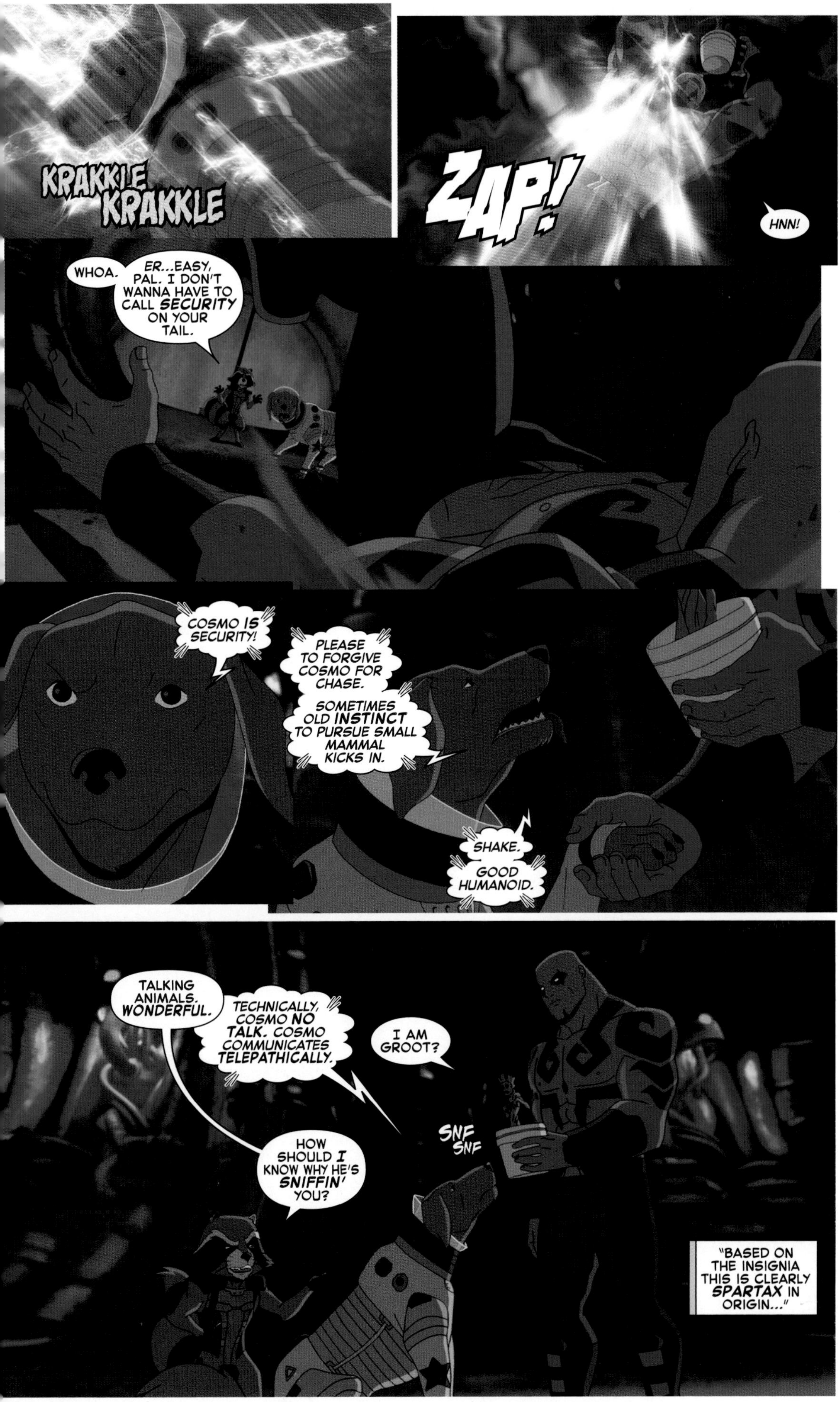
KRAKKLE KRAKKLE
ZAP!
HNN!
WHOA.
ER...EASY, PAL. I DON'T WANNA HAVE TO CALL SECURITY ON YOUR TAIL.
COSMO IS SECURITY!
PLEASE TO FORGIVE COSMO FOR CHASE.
SOMETIMES OLD INSTINCT TO PURSUE SMALL MAMMAL KICKS IN.
SHAKE.
GOOD HUMANOID.
TALKING ANIMALS. WONDERFUL.
TECHNICALLY, COSMO NO TALK. COSMO COMMUNICATES TELEPATHICALLY.
I AM GROOT?
SNF SNF
HOW SHOULD I KNOW WHY HE'S SNIFFIN' YOU?
"BASED ON THE INSIGNIA THIS IS CLEARLY SPARTAX IN ORIGIN..."

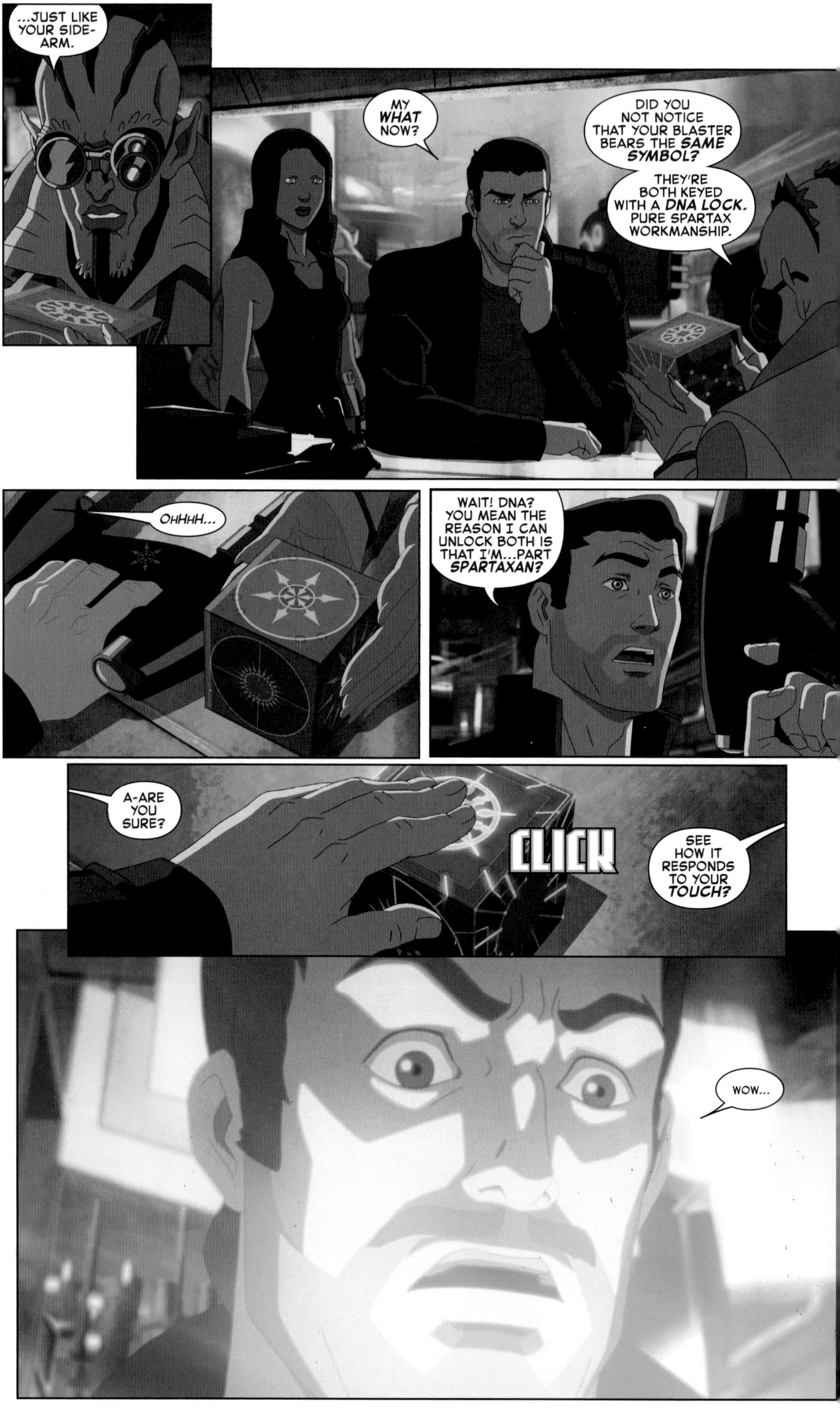
...JUST LIKE YOUR SIDE-ARM.
MY WHAT NOW?
DID YOU NOT NOTICE THAT YOUR BLASTER BEARS THE SAME SYMBOL?
THEY'RE BOTH KEYED WITH A DNA LOCK. PURE SPARTAX WORKMANSHIP.
OHHHH...
WAIT! DNA? YOU MEAN THE REASON I CAN UNLOCK BOTH IS THAT I'M...PART SPARTAXAN?
A-ARE YOU SURE?
CLICK
SEE HOW IT RESPONDS TO YOUR TOUCH?
WOW...

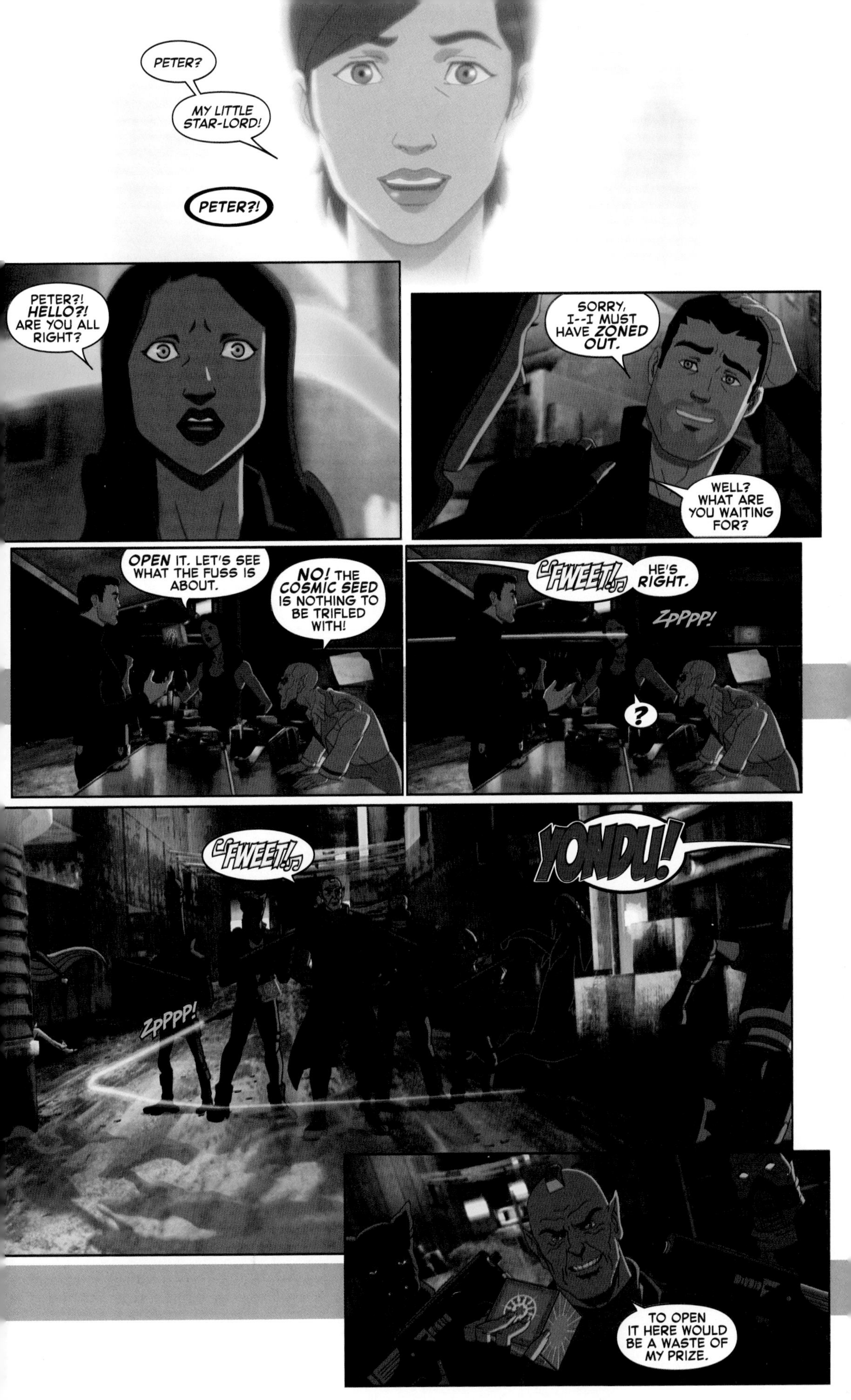
PETER?
MY LITTLE STAR-LORD!
PETER?!
PETER?! HELLO?! ARE YOU ALL RIGHT?
SORRY, I--I MUST HAVE ZONED OUT.
WELL? WHAT ARE YOU WAITING FOR?
OPEN IT. LET'S SEE WHAT THE FUSS IS ABOUT.
NO! THE COSMIC SEED IS NOTHING TO BE TRIFLED WITH!
FWEET!
HE'S RIGHT.
ZPPPP!
?
FWEET!
YONDU!
ZPPPP!
TO OPEN IT HERE WOULD BE A WASTE OF MY PRIZE.

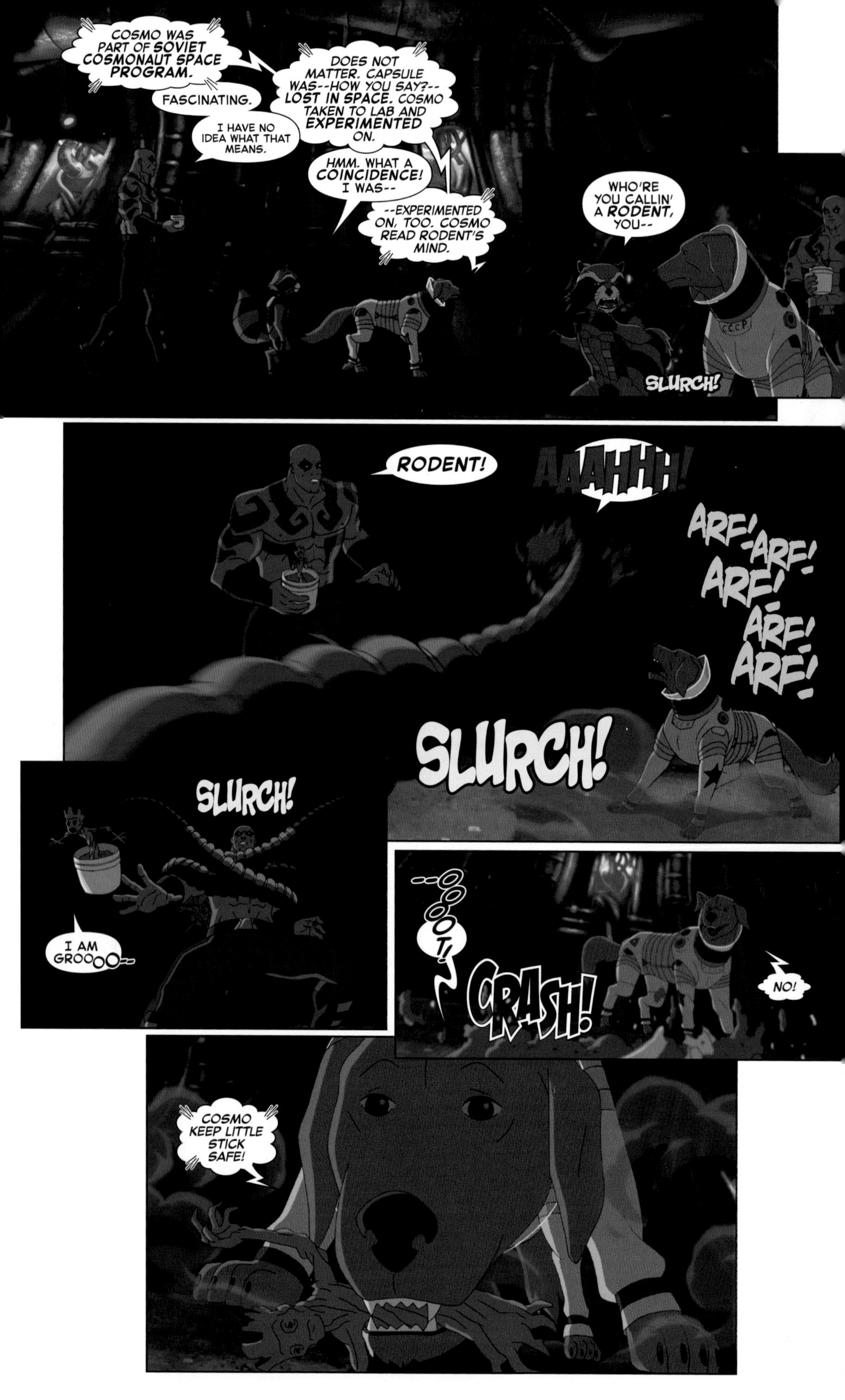
COSMO WAS PART OF SOVIET COSMONAUT SPACE PROGRAM.
FASCINATING.
I HAVE NO IDEA WHAT THAT MEANS.
DOES NOT MATTER. CAPSULE WAS--HOW YOU SAY?--LOST IN SPACE. COSMO TAKEN TO LAB AND EXPERIMENTED ON.
HMM. WHAT A COINCIDENCE! I WAS--
--EXPERIMENTED ON, TOO. COSMO READ RODENT'S MIND.
WHO'RE YOU CALLIN' A RODENT, YOU--
C.C.C.P.
SLURCH!
RODENT!
AAAHHH!
ARF!-ARF!-ARF!-ARF!-ARF!
SLURCH!
SLURCH!
I AM GROOOOO--
--OOOOT!
CRASH!
NO!
COSMO KEEP LITTLE STICK SAFE!

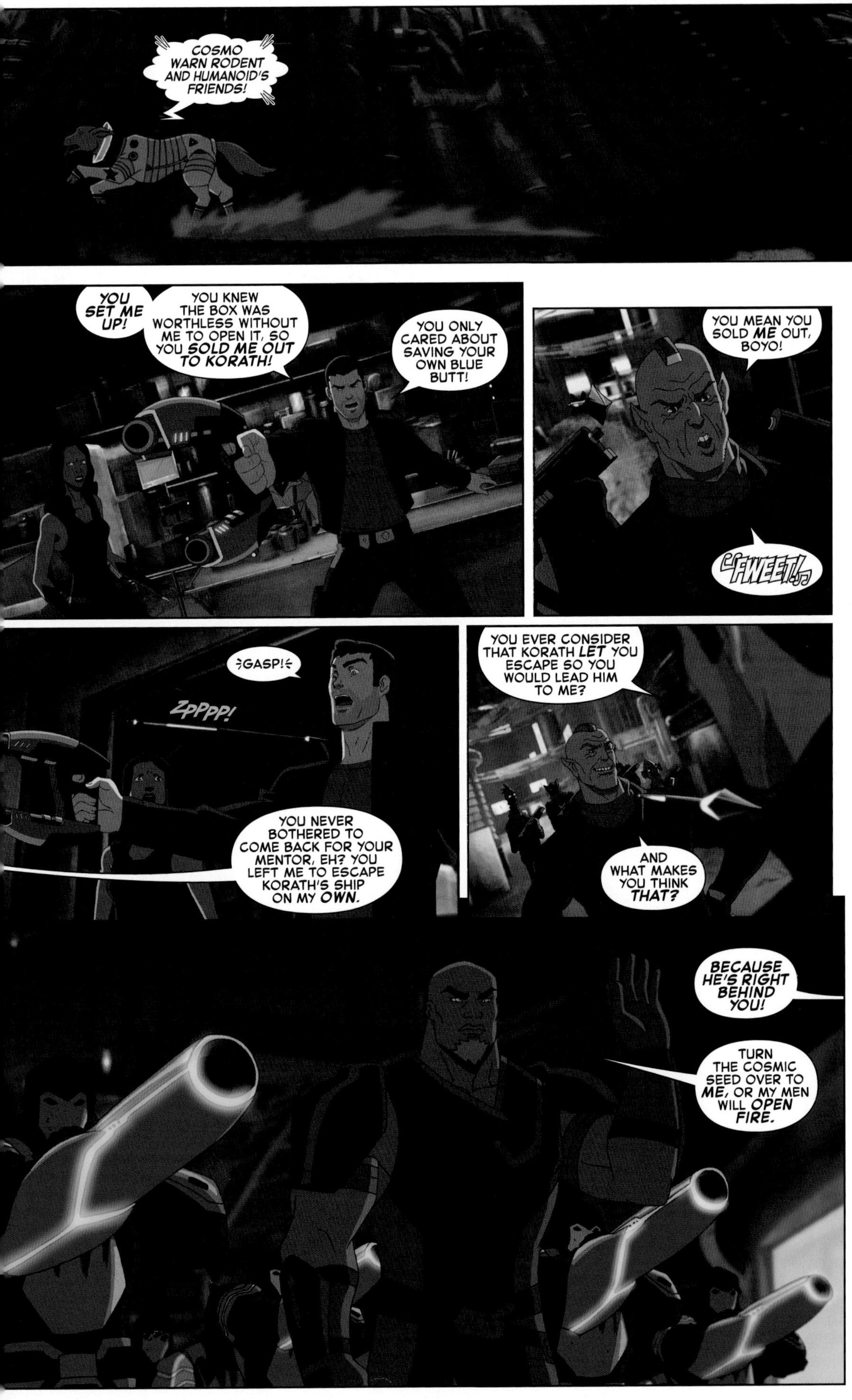
COSMO WARN RODENT AND HUMANOID'S FRIENDS!
YOU SET ME UP!
YOU KNEW THE BOX WAS WORTHLESS WITHOUT ME TO OPEN IT, SO YOU SOLD ME OUT TO KORATH!
YOU ONLY CARED ABOUT SAVING YOUR OWN BLUE BUTT!
YOU MEAN YOU SOLD ME OUT, BOYO!
FWEET!
GASP!
ZPPPP!
YOU NEVER BOTHERED TO COME BACK FOR YOUR MENTOR, EH? YOU LEFT ME TO ESCAPE KORATH'S SHIP ON MY OWN.
YOU EVER CONSIDER THAT KORATH LET YOU ESCAPE SO YOU WOULD LEAD HIM TO ME?
AND WHAT MAKES YOU THINK THAT?
BECAUSE HE'S RIGHT BEHIND YOU!
TURN THE COSMIC SEED OVER TO ME, OR MY MEN WILL OPEN FIRE.

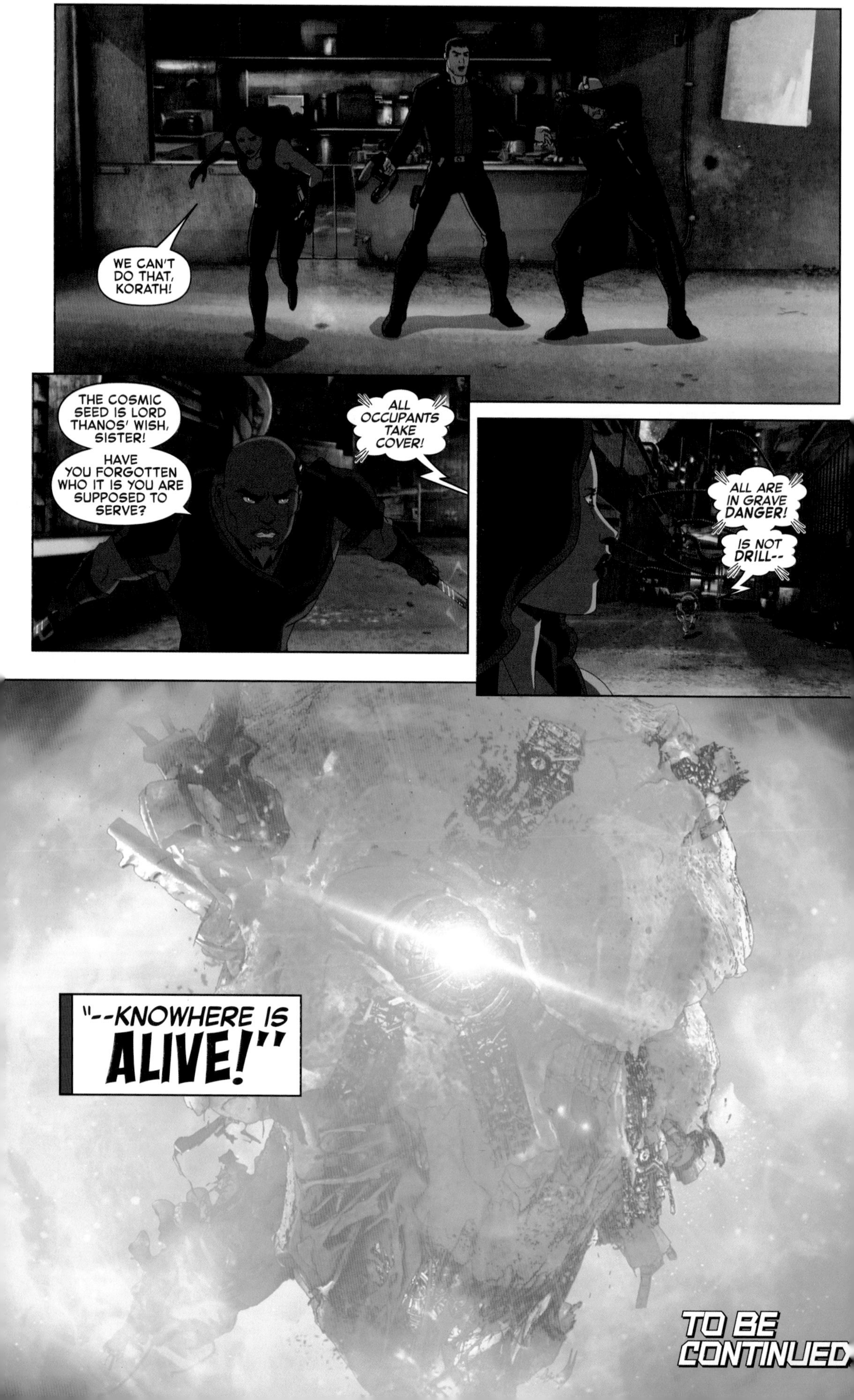
WE CAN'T DO THAT, KORATH!
THE COSMIC SEED IS LORD THANOS' WISH, SISTER!
HAVE YOU FORGOTTEN WHO IT IS YOU ARE SUPPOSED TO SERVE?
ALL OCCUPANTS TAKE COVER!
ALL ARE IN GRAVE DANGER!
IS NOT DRILL--
"--KNOWHERE IS ALIVE!"
TO BE CONTINUED

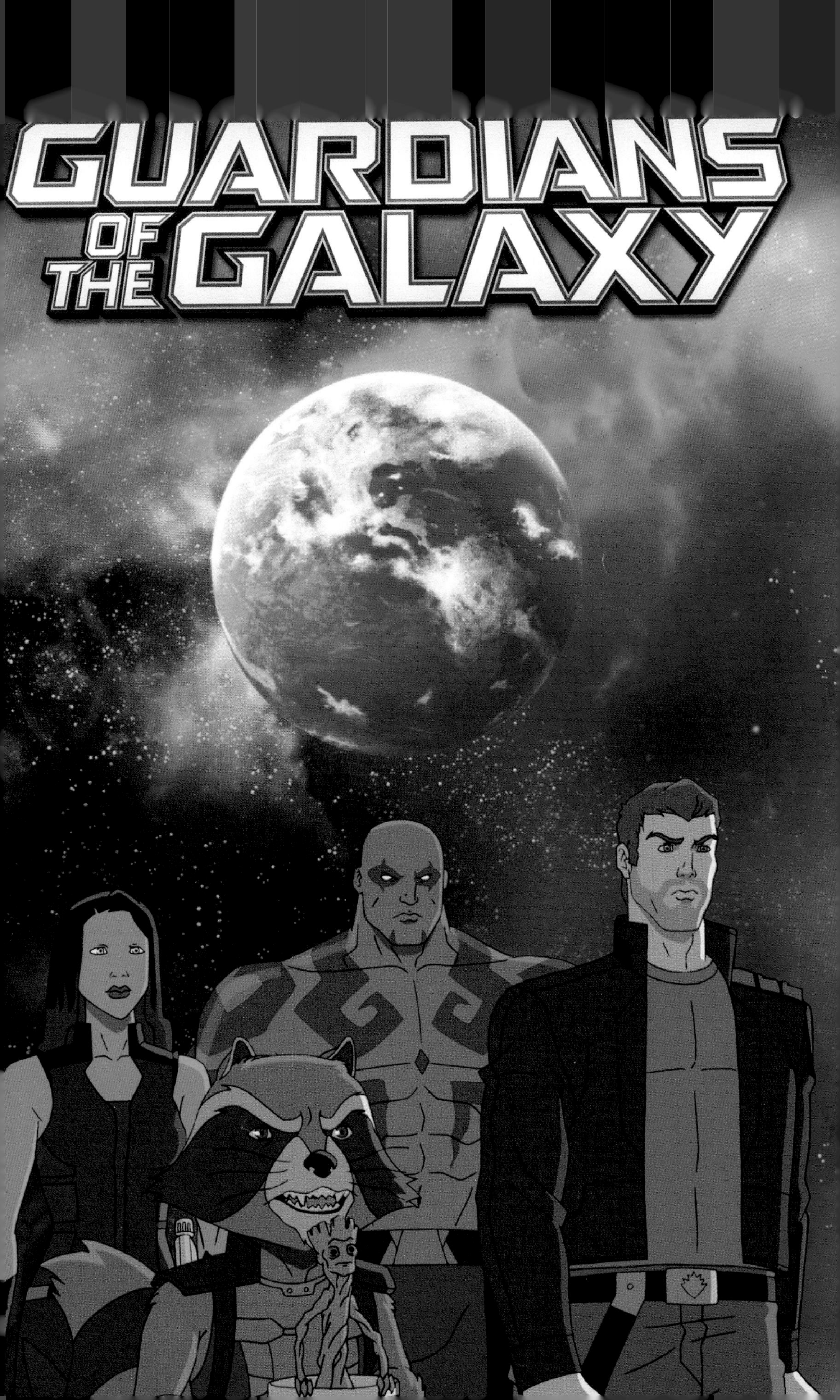
GUARDIANS
OF THE GALAXY

GUARDIANS OF THE GALAXY

COLLECT THEM ALL!

Set of 6 Hardcover Books ISBN: 978-1-5321-4069-3

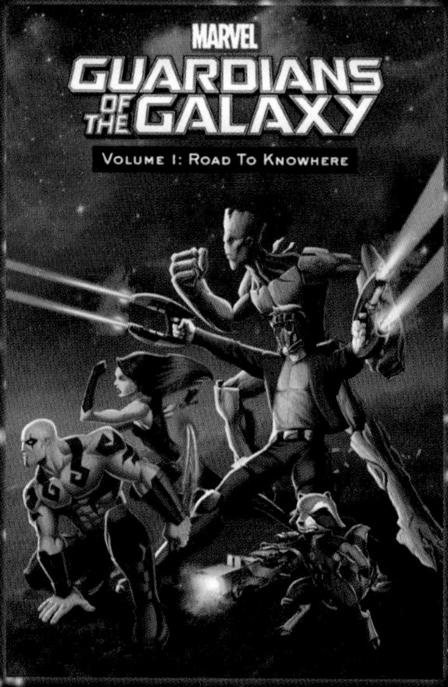
MARVEL
GUARDIANS OF THE GALAXY
Volume 1: Road To Knowhere

Hardcover Book ISBN
978-1-5321-4070-9

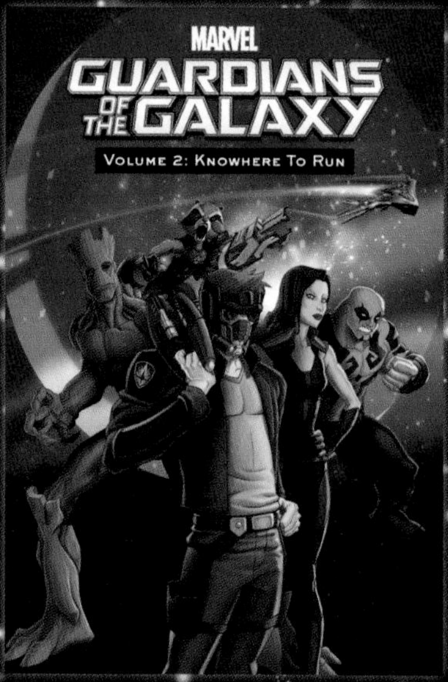
MARVEL
GUARDIANS OF THE GALAXY
Volume 2: Knowhere To Run

Hardcover Book ISBN
978-1-5321-4071-6

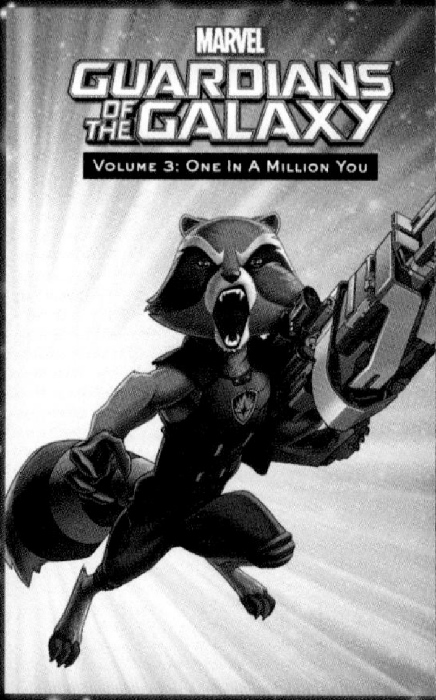
MARVEL
GUARDIANS OF THE GALAXY
Volume 3: One In A Million You

Hardcover Book ISBN
978-1-5321-4072-3

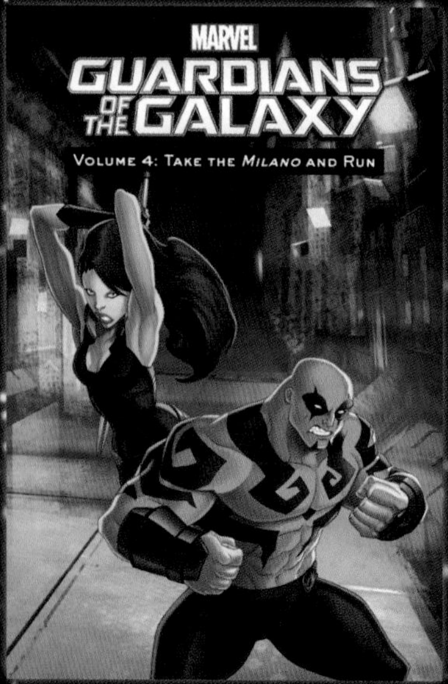
MARVEL
GUARDIANS OF THE GALAXY
Volume 4: Take the *Milano* and Run

Hardcover Book ISBN
978-1-5321-4073-0

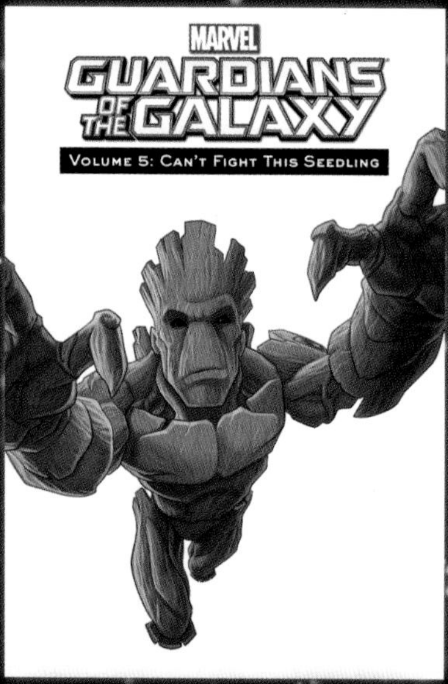
MARVEL
GUARDIANS OF THE GALAXY
Volume 5: Can't Fight This Seedling

Hardcover Book ISBN
978-1-5321-4074-7

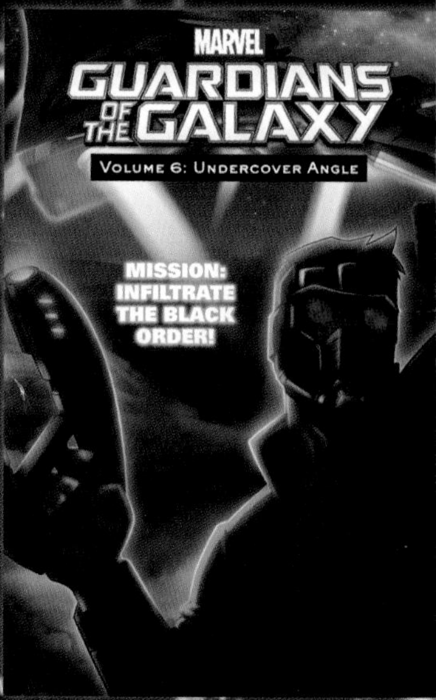
MARVEL
GUARDIANS OF THE GALAXY
Volume 6: Undercover Angle
MISSION: INFILTRATE THE BLACK ORDER!

Hardcover Book ISBN
978-1-5321-4075-4